TEAM SPIRIT ®

SMART BOOKS FOR YOUNG FANS

THE NEW YORK KNICKS

BY
MARK STEWART

NORWOOD HOUSE PRESS
CHICAGO, ILLINOIS

Norwood House Press
P.O. Box 316598
Chicago, Illinois 60631

For information regarding Norwood House Press, please visit our website at:
www.norwoodhousepress.com or call 866-565-2900.

All photos courtesy of Associated Press except the following:
Capitol Cards (6, 38), Black Book Partners (7, 17, 39, 43 right), Author's Collection (11, 33, 43 left),
Bowman Gum Co. (15), Topps, Inc. (18, 21, 26, 34 right, 36, 40, 42 left, 45), New York Knicks (19, 27),
JBC/NBA Hoops (22), SLAM/Source Interlink (31), ESPN, Inc. (35 top right).
Cover Photo: John Minchillo/Associated Press

The memorabilia and artifacts pictured in this book are presented for educational and informational purposes,
and come from the collection of the author.

Editor: Mike Kennedy
Designer: Ron Jaffe
Project Management: Black Book Partners, LLC.
Special thanks to Topps, Inc.

Library of Congress Cataloging-in-Publication Data

Stewart, Mark, 1960 July 7-
    The New York Knicks / by Mark Stewart.
        pages cm. -- (Team spirit)
    Includes bibliographical references and index.
    Summary: "A revised Team Spirit Basketball edition featuring the New York
Knicks that chronicles the history and accomplishments of the team. Includes
access to the Team Spirit website which provides additional information and
photos"-- Provided by publisher.
    ISBN 978-1-59953-638-5 (library edition : alk. paper) -- ISBN
978-1-60357-647-5 (ebook)
    1. New York Knickerbockers (Basketball team)--History--Juvenile
literature. I. Title.
    GV885.52.N4S75 2014
    796.323'64097471--dc23

                                                    2014003847

253N—072014
Manufactured in the United States of America in North Mankato, Minnesota.

COVER PHOTO: The Knicks try to treat their fans to something special every time they take the court.

Table of Contents

ABOUT OUR GLOSSARY

In this book, there may be several words that you are reading for the first time. Some are sports words, some are new vocabulary words, and some are familiar words that are used in an unusual way. All of these words are defined on page 46. Throughout the book, sports words appear in **bold type**. Regular vocabulary words appear in *bold italic type*.

Meet the Knicks

In New York, basketball is considered the "city game." It is played in countless gyms and outdoor courts by thousands of talented young men and women. The New York Knicks are an important part of this picture. When the Knicks are playing well, the entire city is energized. When they are struggling, you can almost feel it on the streets.

The Knicks have built a *tradition* of smart, unselfish basketball. That means setting up teammates for easy shots, helping out on defense, and giving an extra effort on rebounds. Today's players try to live up to the example set by the stars of the past. When they do, the results are spectacular.

This book tells the story of the Knicks. They wear the team's orange and blue colors with a sense of history and pride. Every time the Knicks take the floor, they know that the hopes and dreams of millions of basketball fans are riding on their play.

Iman Shumpert gets some words of encouragement from Amar'e Stoudemire during a 2013–14 game.

Glory Days

New York City's proud basketball tradition stretches back more than a century. In the early part of the 1900s, there were more players and fans in and around the "Big Apple" than in any other part of the country. So when the **Basketball Association of America (BAA)** formed in 1946, people everywhere kept a close eye on the New York Knickerbockers, or "Knicks" for short.

The Knicks turned out to be one of the best teams in the league. They continued their fine play after the BAA joined forces with the older **National Basketball League (NBL)** to form the **National Basketball Association (NBA)**. Much of the credit for New York's success went to the team's coach, Joe Lapchick. He had been a legendary player in the 1920s and a very popular college coach after that. Lapchick demanded that the Knicks play as a team. As a result, New York made it to the **playoffs** in each of Lapchick's eight seasons. They reached the **NBA Finals** three times in a row, from 1950–51 to 1952–53.

The stars of those early clubs included Harry Gallatin, Dick McGuire, Carl Braun, Vince Boryla, Max Zaslofsky, Ray Felix, Connie Simmons, Ernie Vandeweghe, and Nat "Sweetwater" Clifton. Clifton was the first African-American star

in the NBA. In the years that followed, many more good players wore the New York uniform, including Richie Guerin, Kenny Sears, Willie Naulls, and Johnny Green. However, the Knicks fell behind other NBA teams during the late 1950s and early 1960s. At one point, they suffered eight losing seasons in a row.

New York began to rebuild around a group of talented and unselfish players, including college stars Willis Reed, Bill Bradley, Cazzie Russell, Walt Frazier, Phil Jackson, and Dave Stallworth. Trades for Dave DeBusschere, Dick Barnett, Jerry Lucas, and Earl Monroe made the Knicks even better. Under coach Red Holzman,

LEFT: Coach Joe Lapchick turned the Knicks into one of the NBA's best teams.
ABOVE: Dave DeBusschere battles for a loose ball.

they became NBA champions in 1970 and again in 1973.

As these stars retired, the Knicks found other exciting players, including Bob McAdoo, Spencer Haywood, Ray Williams, Micheal Ray Richardson, Bill Cartwright, and Bernard King. The Knicks played winning basketball, but they were never a serious championship **contender**. The team did not return to the NBA Finals until the 1990s.

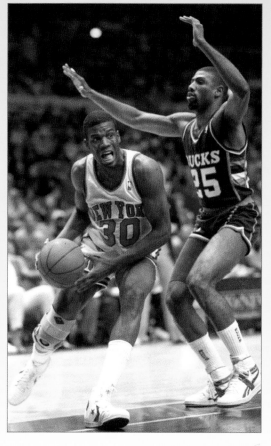

By then, New York had a new coach and a new star. Pat Riley, who guided the Los Angeles Lakers to four championships during the 1980s, was hired to coach the team. Patrick Ewing, a fierce and *agile* center, led a tough, defensive-minded club that featured great supporting players, including Mark Jackson, Charles Oakley, Anthony Mason, and John Starks. Ewing and the Knicks developed a bitter *rivalry* with Michael Jordan and the Chicago Bulls. Unfortunately, New York often came out on the short end of the score when they played. The Knicks finally reached the NBA Finals in 1994, and came within a basket of beating the Houston Rockets for the championship.

LEFT: Most fans agree that Patrick Ewing was the best player in team history.
ABOVE: Bernard King drives to the basket.

In the spring of 1999, the Knicks returned to the NBA Finals. Ewing was still the team leader. His supporting cast now included **All-Stars** Larry Johnson, Allan Houston, and Latrell Sprewell. Once again, New York fell short of the championship, this time losing to the San Antonio Spurs in five games. Ewing played his final season in New York in 1999–2000. He retired as the team's all-time leader in scoring and rebounding.

The team remained competitive after that, but bad luck, poor play, and untimely injuries soon struck the Knicks. New York tried to rebuild by bringing in *veterans* and players that other teams had given up on. Fans had plenty of stars to cheer for, including Stephon Marbury, Eddy Curry, Nate Robinson, Jamal Crawford, Zach Randolph, David Lee, and Al Harrington. Unfortunately, the chemistry on the court was never quite right. New York went nine seasons in a row without a winning record.

The Knicks' fortunes finally began to change in 2010–11. That season, two veteran forwards— Amar'e Stoudemire and Carmelo Anthony— joined the team. Their ability to score and rebound took the pressure off their teammates, who

were free to play supporting roles. The following year, the Knicks hired Mike Woodson to coach the team. He put a greater emphasis on defense, and the victories began piling up. In 2012–13, the Knicks finished atop the **Atlantic Division** for the first time since the 1990s.

The Knicks rediscovered their winning ways thanks to a total team effort. At various times, they got important contributions from Raymond Felton, Tyson Chandler, Iman Shumpert, Steve Novak, and J.R. Smith. These players worked hard and were ready to step up when Anthony and Stoudemire were injured or needed a break. It is that kind of team basketball that wins games, and that kind of commitment that wins championships.

LEFT: Allan Houston and Latrell Sprewell starred for the Knicks when they reached the 1999 NBA Finals.   **ABOVE**: Amar'e Stoudemire, Carmelo Anthony, and Tyson Chandler signed this photo.

Home Court

The Knicks have made their home in two arenas, and both were called Madison Square Garden. They were about a mile apart, on the city's West Side. The team's current "MSG" opened during the 1967–68 season. It is considered America's most famous basketball arena.

In the first Madison Square Garden, the Knicks sometimes took a backseat to more popular events, including hockey games and the circus. When two events were scheduled at once, the Knicks had to find another place to play. Often, they used a local *armory*.

BY THE NUMBERS

- The Knicks' arena has 19,812 seats for basketball.

- As of 2013–14, the Knicks had retired seven numbers: 10 (Walt Frazier), 12 (Dick Barnett), 15 (Earl Monroe & Dick McGuire), 19 (Willis Reed), 22 (Dave DeBusschere), 24 (Bill Bradley), and 33 (Patrick Ewing). The team also retired number 613—the number of games won by coach Red Holzman.

- The Knicks' arena was modernized in 2014 at a cost of $297 million.

The Knicks battle the Miami Heat at Madison Square Garden.

Dressed for Success

The official colors of New York City are orange and blue. Those are also the team colors of the Knicks. For home games, their traditional uniform is white with orange and blue highlights. Their road uniforms are usually blue with orange lettering. In recent years, they have worn several different uniforms, including one that's all orange.

New York got its name from the club's founder, Ned Irish. For almost 20 years, the team's official *logo* showed a colonial New Yorker (or Knickerbocker) dribbling a basketball. The name was shortened to "Knicks" so it could fit on a uniform. In 1964, the Knickerbocker logo was replaced. New York's logo has gone through several changes since then.

LEFT: Andrea Bargnani rises for a jump shot in New York's 2013–14 road uniform.   **ABOVE**: Bud Palmer models the team's home uniform of the 1940s.

A basketball team can look great on paper, but games are won and lost on the court. The Knicks learned this lesson in the spring of 1969, when they lost the championship of the **Eastern Conference** to the aging Boston Celtics. Boston went on to defeat the Los Angeles Lakers in the NBA Finals. The Knicks believed that title should have been theirs.

Coach Red Holzman made sure his team was ready to play in 1969–70. New York's leaders were center Willis Reed, forward Dave DeBusschere, and guard Walt Frazier. They were joined by forwards Bill Bradley, Dave Stallworth, and Cazzie Russell, and guards Dick Barnett and Mike Riordan. Each of these players was good enough to be a star on another team. Their coach taught them how to be part of something much greater.

Holzman urged his players to keep passing the ball until they found an open man. Because everyone on the team could shoot well, the Knicks were very hard to defend. Holzman also taught his team a complicated defense. Often, right in the middle of the

Walt Frazier and Dave Stallworth watch as Cazzie Russell releases a jump shot. Teamwork was the key to New York's success.

action, two New York teammates would "switch" the players they were guarding. This confused the opponent and put less strain on the defense.

The Knicks won 60 games during the 1969–70 season—more than any other team in the NBA. They beat the Baltimore Bullets in a tough first-round playoff series. Next, New York faced the Milwaukee Bucks and their 7' 2" center, Kareem Abdul-Jabbar. Reed battled Abdul-Jabbar one-on-one, while the rest of the Knicks

1969·70 NBA championship photo album

"World Champs"

knicks win it!

outplayed the Bucks. New York won the series easily.

The Knicks met the Lakers in the NBA Finals. Reed faced another great center in Wilt Chamberlain, and again he held his own. With New York leading the series, Reed injured his leg. Chamberlain took advantage, and the Lakers forced a decisive Game 7. It looked like all was lost for New York, but to everyone's surprise, Reed limped onto the court. His presence provided the spark in a 113–99 victory. All of New York celebrated the Knicks' first NBA championship.

The Knicks and Lakers squared off again in the 1972 NBA Finals. This time Los Angeles won. At the end of the following season, the two teams met for the championship for a third time. The Knicks were an even more dangerous team after adding All-Stars Earl Monroe and Jerry Lucas. Like the other Knicks, they found roles that gave New York the best chance to win.

Reed was healthy for the entire NBA Finals in 1973. He made Chamberlain work hard for every shot and every rebound. Meanwhile, the rest of the team played brilliant defense. The Lakers won the opening game, 115–112. New York put the clamps on Los Angeles from that point on. The Knicks swept the next four games to win their second championship.

The Knicks reached the NBA Finals again in 1994. They were led by another great center, Patrick Ewing. New York faced the Houston Rockets in a thrilling series that went seven games. Unfortunately, the Knicks lost the championship in a close game on Houston's home court. Five years later, the Knicks returned to the NBA Finals. This time, they were defeated by the San Antonio Spurs.

LEFT: This trading card shows the Knicks celebrating their first NBA title.
ABOVE: Earl Monroe battles Jerry West of the Lakers on the cover of the team's 1973 yearbook.

Go-To Guys

To be a true star in the NBA, you need more than a great shot. You have to be a "go-to guy"—someone teammates trust to make the winning play when the seconds are ticking away in a big game. Knicks fans have had a lot to cheer about over the years, including these great stars ...

THE PIONEERS

DICK McGUIRE   6′ 6″ Guard

• BORN: 1/25/1926   • DIED: 2/3/2010   • PLAYED FOR TEAM: 1949–50 TO 1956–57

Dick McGuire was nicknamed "Tricky Dick" for his lightning-fast dribbling and quick passes. He led the Knicks to the NBA Finals three seasons in a row. McGuire entered the **Hall of Fame** in 1993.

RICHIE GUERIN   6′ 4″ Guard

• BORN 5/29/1932   • PLAYED FOR TEAM: 1956–57 TO 1963–64

Richie Guerin played guard but scored and rebounded like a big man. He was almost impossible to defend. Guerin averaged more than 20 points a game four seasons in a row, including a 29.5 scoring average in 1961–62.

WILLIS REED   6′ 10″ Center

- BORN: 6/25/1942   • PLAYED FOR TEAM: 1964–65 TO 1973–74

Willis Reed was a great all-around star. Few centers were as *versatile*. His shooting, rebounding, defense, and leadership helped the Knicks win their first two NBA championships.

WALT FRAZIER   6′ 4″ Guard

- BORN: 3/29/1945   • PLAYED FOR TEAM: 1967–68 TO 1976–77

Walt Frazier had style on and off the court. He was a big, strong guard who was also very fast and quick. Frazier was an excellent shooter and ball handler, and one of the best defensive players in the NBA.

DAVE DeBUSSCHERE   6′ 6″ Forward

- BORN: 10/16/1940   • DIED: 5/14/2003   • PLAYED FOR TEAM: 1968–69 TO 1973–74

Dave DeBusschere was the final ingredient in New York's rise to the NBA championship. He was a skilled defender and rebounder, and had an excellent jump shot. In DeBusschere's first full season with the Knicks, they won their first NBA title.

EARL MONROE   6′ 3″ Guard

- BORN: 11/21/1944

- PLAYED FOR TEAM: 1971–72 TO 1979–80

Earl Monroe was nicknamed "The Pearl." He was the NBA's flashiest player before he joined the Knicks. Monroe changed his style to fit in with the Knicks and helped them win the NBA championship in 1973.

RIGHT: Earl Monroe

BERNARD KING   6′ 7″ Forward

- BORN: 12/4/1956   • PLAYED FOR TEAM: 1982–83 TO 1986–87

Bernard King was one of the NBA's truly "unstoppable" scorers. He released his shot so quickly that defenders had no chance of blocking it. In 1984–85, he became the first Knick to lead the NBA in scoring.

PATRICK EWING   7′ 0″ Center

- BORN: 8/5/1962   • PLAYED FOR TEAM: 1985–86 TO 1999–2000

Patrick Ewing was a *dominant* defender in college. When he joined the Knicks, he proved he was an equally talented scorer. Ewing's leadership helped the Knicks reach the NBA Finals twice. He was an All-Star 12 times.

CHARLES OAKLEY   6′ 8″ Forward

- BORN: 12/18/1963
- PLAYED FOR TEAM: 1988–89 TO 1997–98

Charles Oakley was one of the hardest working players in the NBA. When a ball was loose anywhere near "Oak," chances were good that it would end up in his hands. Oakley was an excellent rebounder and one of the NBA's best defensive players.

ABOVE: Charles Oakley   **RIGHT**: Carmelo Anthony

JOHN STARKS — 6′ 3″ Guard

- BORN: 8/10/1965 • PLAYED FOR TEAM: 1990–91 TO 1997–98

John Starks played for four different colleges and three **professional** teams before he came to the Knicks. He finally found his basketball home in New York. Starks played with great heart and became a fan favorite in Madison Square Garden.

ALLAN HOUSTON — 6′ 6″ Guard

- BORN: 4/20/1971 • PLAYED FOR TEAM: 1996–97 TO 2004–05

Allan Houston was a deadly accurate shooter. As the son of a college basketball coach, he had a great understanding of the game. Houston teamed up with Latrell Sprewell to give the Knicks a dangerous one-two scoring punch.

CARMELO ANTHONY — 6′ 8″ Forward

- BORN: 5/29/1984
- FIRST SEASON WITH TEAM: 2010–11

The Knicks traded for Carmelo Anthony because they wanted a player who could score from any spot on the floor. In 2011–12, he set a team record with 20 or more points in 31 games in a row. The following season, Anthony led the NBA with an average of 28.7 points per game.

Calling the Shots

Four coaches have led the Knicks to the NBA Finals. The first was Joe Lapchick. Long before there was an NBA, he starred for a team called the New York Celtics. They traveled all over the country to help promote the sport of basketball. With Lapchick calling the shots, the Knicks reached the NBA Finals each year from 1951 to 1953.

Red Holzman led the Knicks to the NBA Finals three times in the 1970s, and the team won the championship twice. Holzman found ways to mix old-time *strategies* with modern playing styles. In an *era* when most players focused on scoring, he convinced the Knicks to pass the ball on offense and work together on defense. Holzman won more than 600 games in New York.

In 1994, the Knicks went to the NBA Finals under Pat Riley. Riley had coached the Los Angeles Lakers in the 1980s when the team was known for its fast-paced "Showtime" style. In New York, he taught his players to slow the game down. The Knicks relied on strength and toughness to *intimidate* opponents and win games.

Jeff Van Gundy took over for Riley in 1995, Four years later, he guided the Knicks to the NBA Finals. Van Gundy was a shy, quiet man, but he taught his players to be extra aggressive at all times. Under Van Gundy, the Knicks were one of the league's most frustrating teams to face.

In 2014, the Knicks hired Phil Jackson as team president. Jackson began his NBA career in New York and was a member of the 1973 championship team. He went on to coach the Chicago Bulls and the Lakers to 11 titles. Jackson turned Michael Jordan and Kobe Bryant into championship leaders. The Knicks brought Jackson aboard hoping he could do the same for their high-scoring star, Carmelo Anthony.

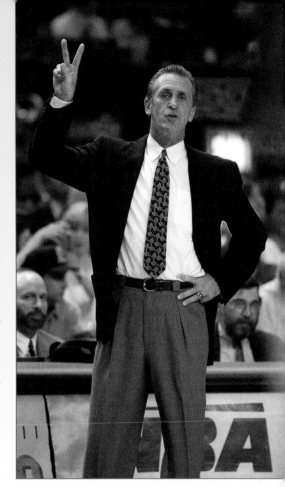

LEFT: Red Holzman won more games than any coach in team history.
ABOVE: Pat Riley calls a play from the sidelines.

One Great Day

There aren't any shortcuts to winning an NBA championship. No one had to tell this to Willis Reed. On the way to New York's first title, the 6' 10" center had to outplay three Hall of Famers—and overcome a crippling injury. Reed and the Knicks

WILLIS REED
center

NEW YORK

began the 1970 playoffs against Wes Unseld and the Baltimore Bullets. Next, they had to face Kareem Abdul-Jabbar of the Milwaukee Bucks. By the time New York met Wilt Chamberlain and the Los Angeles Lakers in the NBA Finals, Reed was exhausted. Nevertheless, he kept Chamberlain under control, and the Knicks won two of the first four games.

In Game 5, disaster struck. Reed tore a muscle in his leg and fell to the floor in agony. The Knicks won the game, but they lost their most important player. Without a big man to guard Chamberlain,

New York was helpless. The Los Angeles star scored 45 points in Game 6, as the Lakers beat the Knicks badly, 135–113.

Game 7 was set for Madison Square Garden. New York fans had little hope that their Knicks would win. The players on both teams seemed to feel this way. But right before tip-off, Reed trotted into the arena. The crowd went crazy. Reed's teammates fed off that energy. The Lakers just stared in disbelief.

WALT FRAZIER

Reed could barely move, but he scored the first basket of the game over Chamberlain. On defense, he used his body to keep the Los Angeles center away from the basket. The rest of the Knicks came to the aid of their leader, especially Walt Frazier. He played one of the best all-around games ever in the NBA Finals with 36 points and 19 **assists**. The Knicks won the championship, and Reed was named the series **Most Valuable Player (MVP)**.

LEFT: Willis Reed's inspirational Game 7 performance helped make him MVP of the 1970 NBA Finals.   **ABOVE**: Walt Frazier was sensational in the win over the Lakers.

Legend Has It

Was Walt Frazier the most fashionable player in the NBA?

LEGEND HAS IT that he was. Frazier was the best-dressed athlete in New York. He loved to wear stylish suits, overcoats, and wide-brimmed hats. Frazier was nicknamed "Clyde" after the notorious Clyde Barrow of Bonnie and Clyde. He was often pictured in magazines and newspapers wearing the most fashionable clothes around.

ABOVE: Walt Frazier shows off the fashion sense that helped earn him the nickname "Clyde."

LEGEND HAS IT that Trent Tucker did. In a 1989–90 game, Tucker received a pass with 0.1 seconds left on the clock and made a **3-pointer** for the victory. Afterwards, the NBA made a new rule that a shot could not be attempted with less than 0.3 seconds on the clock. More than a *decade* later, in a double-**overtime** game, the Knicks got the ball with clock reading 0:00.1. Jamal Crawford threw an inbounds pass high above the rim to David Lee, who flicked the ball with his fingers—right into the basket—as the final buzzer sounded. The basket counted because it was off a deflection, not a shot.

ho gave Knicks fans their greatest hristmas present?

LEGEND HAS IT that Bernard King did. On December 25, 1984, the Knicks played the New Jersey Nets in Madison Square Garden. Neither team had a winning record, so the fans weren't expecting much. King was on fire from start to finish. He made 19 of his 30 shots and added 22 free throws. The Nets won the game, but New York fans were the real winners—they had seen the first 60-point game in team history.

How does an NBA team survive when its two biggest stars are hurt? Usually, it doesn't. That is why New York fans prepared for the worst when Carmelo Anthony and Amar'e Stoudemire were injured in February of 2012. The rest of the Knicks expected the worst, too. They played poorly when the team needed them to play their best.

Coach Mike D'Antoni was so frustrated that he looked down to the end of the bench and decided to give Jeremy Lin a chance. Lin was in his second season and had little experience. In a game against the New Jersey Nets, he went head-to-head with All-Star guard Deron Williams and led the Knicks to a 99–92 win. He scored a career-high 25 points. The next game, against the Utah Jazz, Lin had 28 points in a 99–88 victory. He had 23 points and 10 assists in the next game, as the Knicks beat the Washington Wizards.

Lin's biggest test came in a home game against the Los Angeles Lakers. Superstar Kobe Bryant predicted he would bring the rising star back down to earth. Imagine his surprise when Lin scored 38 points against him in another victory!

Jeremy Lin was front-page news during his amazing run with the Knicks in 2012.

New York City was gripped by "Lin-sanity." He was all anyone could talk about. How could a guy that no one had ever heard of be playing like a Hall of Famer? Not even Lin himself could answer this question.

Three days after beating the Lakers, Lin nailed a 3-pointer at the buzzer against the Toronto Raptors to deliver another thrilling win. That gave him at least 20 points and seven assists in each of his first five NBA starts. No one in league history had done that before.

Lin had another great game against the Dallas Mavericks. The Mavs tried every defense they could think of, but Lin still racked up 28 points and 14 assists in a 104–97 win. Lin's amazing run finally ended with a knee injury. After the season, he left New York to play for the Houston Rockets. Lin appeared in only 26 games for the Knicks, but they were 26 games that no one will ever forget.

K

nicks fans may be the most knowledgeable in the NBA. When they shout advice to the players, or when they criticize them, they usually know what they're talking about. Knicks fans have good memories, too. They don't forget New York's greatest victories—or their worst losses.

The stands at Madison Square Garden are always filled with famous people. New York is home to politicians, authors, actors, artists, and athletes—and many root for the Knicks in courtside seats. The most famous fan in Madison Square Garden is movie director Spike Lee.

KNICKERBOCKERS vs PHILADELPHIA
NEW YORK CELTICS vs. GLOBETROTTERS
X A V I E R   v s .   S T .   A N N ' S
MADISON SQUARE GARDEN   JANUARY 1, 1950
24c. N. Y. C. SALES TAX 1c **25c**

He loves to *heckle* opposing players, and no one celebrates more when the Knicks win.

LEFT: Spike Lee leads the cheers from his courtside seat.   **ABOVE**: As this program shows, basketball-crazy New York fans in the 1950s sometimes saw three games for the price of a single ticket.

The basketball season is played from October through June. That means each season takes place at the end of one year and the beginning of the next. In this timeline, the accomplishments of the Knicks are shown by season.

1950–51
The Knicks reach the NBA Finals for the first time.

1969–70
The Knicks win their first NBA championship.

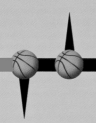

1946–47
The Knicks play their first BAA season.

1968–69
The Knicks trade for Dave DeBusschere.

1972–73
New York wins its second championship.

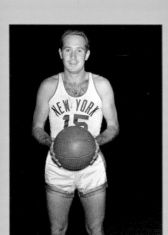

Dick McGuire was a key player on the 1950–51 team.

Jerry Lucas helped the Knicks win the title in 1972–73.

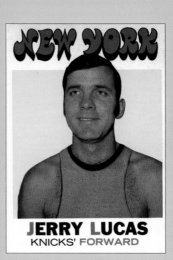

JERRY LUCAS
KNICKS' FORWARD

Anthony
Mason

Carmelo
Anthony

1984–85
Bernard King leads
the NBA in scoring.

1994–95
Anthony Mason wins
the **Sixth Man Award**.

2012–13
Carmelo Anthony leads
the league in scoring.

1985–86
Patrick Ewing is named
Rookie of the Year.

2005–06
Nate Robinson wins the
Slam Dunk contest.

2011–12
Tyson Chandler is
named Defensive
Player of the Year.

Nate Robinson
soars to the basket
during the 2006
Slam Dunk contest.

Fun Facts

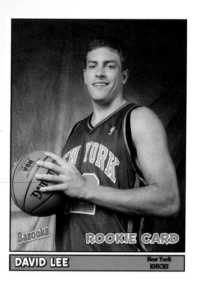

DAVID LEE   New York KNICKS

DAVID AND GOLIATH

In a 2010 game against the Golden State Warriors, 6' 9" David Lee had 37 points, 20 rebounds, and 10 assists. It was the first time in 34 years that a player had reached the 35-20-10 level in a game. The last player to do so was 7' 2" Kareem Abdul-Jabbar.

GROUND BREAKER

Willie Naulls was named captain of the Knicks in the 1950s. He became the team's first African American captain, and the first African American captain in any of the four major professional sports.

FAMOUS FIRST

The Knicks played in the first game in the history of the Basketball Association of America. They faced the Toronto Huskies in Canada. New York won the contest, 68–66.

FEELING BUBBLY

One of the Knicks' first All-Stars was center Nat Clifton. He was nicknamed "Sweetwater" because of his love for soda pop.

RUNNING THE TABLE

In a 1972 game against the Milwaukee Bucks, the Knicks trailed 86–68 in the fourth quarter. They scored 19 straight points to win 87–86. It was the greatest comeback in NBA history.

HOOFING IT

Everyone knew that Kenny "Sky" Walker could jump. He won the Slam Dunk contest as a member of the Knicks in 1989. Three years earlier, Walker proved how fast he was by beating a trotting horse named Pugwash in a 110-yard sprint at Yonkers Raceway.

LEFT: David Lee
ABOVE: Nat "Sweetwater" Clifton leaps high to block a shot.

Talking Basketball

"I could score, but I loved rebounding with a passion."

▶ **Bernard King,** *on the skill that many fans overlooked*

"If the ball was up for grabs, I wanted my share."

▶ **Harry Gallatin,** *on how he led the NBA in rebounds*

"If we win playing ugly ball, we'll take it."

▶ **Carmelo Anthony,** *on winning tough defensive battles*

"Go for the moon. If you don't get it, you'll still be heading for a star."

▶ **Willis Reed,** *on aiming high on and off the court*

"When I was there, it was one of the greatest times to be in New York."

► **Phil Jackson,** *on playing for the Knicks in the 1970s*

"Red would get in your face, but not in the press."

► **Walt Frazier,** *on the respect Red Holzman had for his players*

"As long as you're doing your level best, the people here—whether they are your teammates or the fans—will respect you."

► **Willie Naulls,** *on the key to success in New York*

"The greatest players fit with the team. They play within the team's style, rather than asking the team to change its style."

► **Patrick Ewing,** *on what it takes to win a championship*

LEFT: Harry Gallatin
ABOVE: Phil Jackson blocks a shot against the Los Angeles Lakers.

Great Debates

People who root for the Knicks love to compare their favorite moments, teams, and players. Some debates have been going on for years! How would you settle these classic basketball arguments?

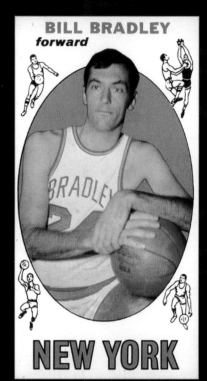

BILL BRADLEY
forward

NEW YORK

No Knick was smarter than Bill Bradley ...

... because he devoted his life to learning. After graduating from Princeton University, Bradley (LEFT) was awarded a *scholarship* to the University of Oxford in England. After his Hall of Fame career as a player, Bradley went into politics. He was elected to the U.S. Senate, and later Bradley tried to become President of the United States.

Forget it. Jerry Lucas was the smartest Knick ...

... because he was a professional memory expert. His goal was to unlock the "power of the mind" by exercising his brain the way other players exercised their bodies. After retiring from the NBA, Lucas wrote several books and taught people around the country how to increase their brainpower.

. . . because it helped the Knicks reach the NBA Finals. New York trailed the Indiana Pacers by three points with six seconds left. As Johnson attempted a 3-pointer, he was fouled by Antonio Davis.

The shot went in, and Johnson made his free throw to win the game, 92–91. The Knicks went on to take the **Eastern Conference Finals** in six games.

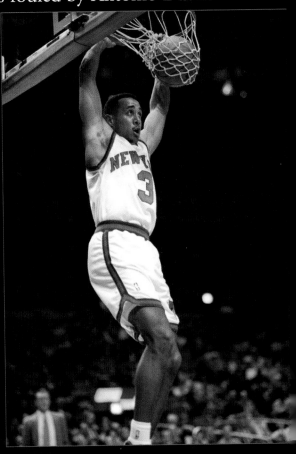

John Starks might have something to say about that . . .

. . . because fans still ask him about his dunk against the Chicago Bulls. It happened in the final moments of Game 2 of a playoff series in 1993. Starks (RIGHT) saw an opening in the Chicago defense and attacked the rim with three Bulls—including Michael Jordan—waiting for him. Starks soared over all of them and scored on a violent, left-handed dunk to seal New York's victory.

For the Record

The great Knicks teams and players have left their marks on the record books. These are the "best of the best" …

Walt Frazier

KNICKS AWARD WINNERS

ROOKIE OF THE YEAR
Willis Reed	1964–65
Patrick Ewing	1985–86

ALL-STAR GAME MVP
Willis Reed	1969–70
Walt Frazier	1974–75

NBA FINALS MVP
Willis Reed	1969–70
Willis Reed	1972–73

COACH OF THE YEAR
Red Holzman	1969–70
Pat Riley	1992–93

NBA MVP
Willis Reed	1969–70

SLAM DUNK CHAMPION
Kenny Walker	1988–89
Nate Robinson	2005–06
Nate Robinson	2008–09

SIXTH MAN AWARD
Anthony Mason	1994–95
John Starks	1996–97
J.R. Smith	2012–13

DEFENSIVE PLAYER OF THE YEAR
Tyson Chandler	2011–12

Willis Reed, Patrick Ewing, and Dave DeBusschere share a laugh together.

KNICKS ACHIEVEMENTS

ACHIEVEMENT	YEAR
Eastern Division Champions	1950–51
Eastern Division Champions	1951–52
Eastern Division Champions	1952–53
Eastern Division Champions	1969–70
NBA Champions	1969–70
Atlantic Division Champions	1970–71
Eastern Conference Champions	1971–72
Eastern Conference Champions	1972–73
NBA Champions	1972–73
Atlantic Division Champions	1988–89
Atlantic Division Champions	1992–93
Atlantic Division Champions	1993–94
Eastern Conference Champions	1993–94
Eastern Conference Champions	1998–99
Atlantic Division Champions	2012–13

ABOVE: Earl Monroe flips up a shot. He was a star for the 1973 champs.
LEFT: J.R. Smith signed this photo of him dunking.

Pinpoints

The history of a basketball team is made up of many smaller stories. These stories take place all over the map—not just in the city a team calls "home." Match the pushpins on these maps to the **TEAM FACTS**, and you will begin to see the story of the Knicks unfold!

TEAM FACTS

1 New York, New York—*The Knicks have played here since the 1946–47 season.*

2 Philadelphia, Pennsylvania—*Earl Monroe was born here.*

3 Cleveland, Ohio—*Charles Oakley was born here.*

4 Louisville, Kentucky—*Allan Houston was born here.*

5 Detroit, Michigan—*Dave DeBusschere was born here.*

6 Dallas, Texas—*Willie Naulls was born here.*

7 Los Angeles, California—*Jeremy Lin was born here.*

8 Atlanta, Georgia—*Walt Frazier was born here.*

9 Hico, Louisiana—*Willis Reed was born here.*

10 Tulsa, Oklahoma—*John Starks was born here.*

11 Rome, Italy—*Andrea Bargnani was born here.*

12 Kingston, Jamaica—*Patrick Ewing was born here.*

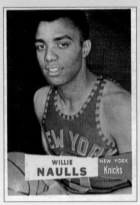

Willie Naulls

Glossary

🏀 Basketball Words
🧠 Vocabulary Words

🏀 **3-POINTER**—A basket made from behind the 3-point line.

🧠 **AGILE**—Quick and graceful.

🏀 **ALL-STARS**—Players selected to play in the annual All-Star Game.

🧠 **ARMORY**—A building where military equipment is stored.

🏀 **ASSISTS**—Passes that lead to baskets.

🏀 **ATLANTIC DIVISION**—A group of teams that play in a region that is close to the Atlantic Ocean.

🏀 **BASKETBALL ASSOCIATION OF AMERICA (BAA)**—The league that started in 1946–47 and later became the NBA.

🏀 **CONTENDER**—A team that competes for a championship.

🧠 **DECADE**—A period of 10 years; also specific periods, such as the 1950s.

🧠 **DOMINANT**—Overpowering.

🏀 **EASTERN CONFERENCE**—A group of teams that play in the East. The winner of the Eastern Conference meets the winner of the Western Conference in the league finals.

🏀 **EASTERN CONFERENCE FINALS**—The playoff series that determines which team from the East will play in the NBA Finals.

🧠 **ERA**—A period of time in history.

🏀 **HALL OF FAME**—The museum in Springfield, Massachusetts where basketball's greatest players are honored. A player voted into the Hall of Fame is sometimes called a "Hall of Famer."

🧠 **HECKLE**—Provoke or make fun of.

🧠 **INTIMIDATE**—Scare or frighten.

🧠 **LOGO**—A symbol or design that represents a company or team.

🏀 **MOST VALUABLE PLAYER (MVP)**—The annual award given to the league's best player; also given to the best player in the league finals and All-Star Game.

🏀 **NATIONAL BASKETBALL ASSOCIATION (NBA)**—The professional league that has been operating since 1946–47.

🏀 **NATIONAL BASKETBALL LEAGUE (NBL)**—An early professional league that played from 1937–38 to 1948–49.

🏀 **NBA FINALS**—The playoff series that decides the champion of the league.

🏀 **OVERTIME**—The extra period played when a game is tied after 48 minutes.

🏀 **PLAYOFFS**—The games played after the season to determine the league champion.

🏀 **PROFESSIONAL**—A player or team that plays a sport for money.

🧠 **RIVALRY**—Extremely emotional competition.

🏀 **ROOKIE OF THE YEAR**—The annual award given to the league's best first-year player.

🧠 **SCHOLARSHIP**—Financial aid given to a student.

🏀 **SIXTH MAN AWARD**—The annual award given to the league's best player off the bench.

🧠 **STRATEGIES**—Plans for succeeding.

🧠 **TRADITION**—A belief or custom that is handed down from generation to generation.

🧠 **VERSATILE**—Able to do many things well.

🧠 **VETERANS**—Players with great experience.

FAST BREAK

TEAM SPIRIT introduces a great way to stay up to date with your team! Visit our **FAST BREAK** link and get connected to the latest and greatest updates. **FAST BREAK** serves as a young reader's ticket to an exclusive web page—with more stories, fun facts, team records, and photos of the Knicks. Content is updated during and after each season. The **FAST BREAK** feature also enables readers to send comments and letters to the author! Log onto:

www.norwoodhousepress.com/library.aspx

and click on the tab: **TEAM SPIRIT** to access **FAST BREAK**.

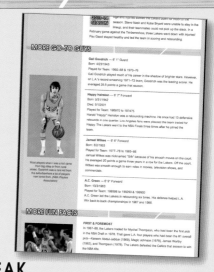

Read all the books in the series to learn more about professional sports. For a complete listing of the baseball, basketball, football, and hockey teams in the **TEAM SPIRIT** series, visit our website at:

www.norwoodhousepress.com/library.aspx

On the Road

NEW YORK KNICKS
Two Pennsylvania Plaza
New York, New York 10121
(212) 465-6000
www.nyknicks.com

**NAISMITH MEMORIAL
BASKETBALL HALL OF FAME**
1000 West Columbus Avenue
Springfield, Massachusetts 01105
(877) 4HOOPLA
www.hoophall.com

On the Bookshelf

To learn more about the sport of basketball, look for these books at your library or bookstore:

- Doeden, Matt. *Basketball Legends In the Making*. North Mankato, Minnesota: Capstone Press, 2014.

- Rappaport, Ken. *Basketball's Top 10 Slam Dunkers*. Berkeley Heights, New Jersey: Enslow Publishers, 2013.

- Silverman, Drew. *The NBA Finals*. Minneapolis, Minnesota: ABDO Group, 2013.

47

Index

THE TEAM

MARK STEWART has written more than 40 books on basketball, and over 150 sports books for kids. He grew up in New York City during the 1960s rooting for the Knicks and Nets, and was lucky enough to meet many of the stars of those teams. Mark comes from a family of writers. His grandfather was Sunday Editor of *The New York Times* and his mother was Articles Editor of *The Ladies' Home Journal* and *McCall's*. Mark has profiled hundreds of athletes over the last 20 years. He has also written several books about his native New York, and New Jersey, his home today. Mark is a graduate of Duke University, with a degree in History. He lives with his daughters and wife Sarah overlooking Sandy Hook, New Jersey.